They took some honey,

and plenty of money,

Wrapped up in a five-pound note.

The Owl looked up to the stars above

And sang to a small guitar —

'O lovely Pussy, O Pussy, my love,

What a beautiful Pussy you are,

you are, you are,

What a beautiful Pussy you are!'

Pussy said to the Owl,

'You elegant fowl,

How charmingly sweet you sing!

O let us be married,

Too long we have tarried,

But what shall we do for a ring?'

The Owl and the Pussycat went to sea

In a beautiful pea-green boat.

The Owl and the Pussycat

Edward Lear

Illustrated by Wendy Straw

They sailed away for a year and a day,

To the land where the bong-tree grows,

And there in the wood a Piggy-wig stood,

With a ring at the end of his nose, his nose, his nose,

With a ring at the end of his nose.

'Dear Pig, are you willing

To sell for one shilling,

Your ring?'

Said the Piggy, 'I will.'

So they took it away, and were married next day

By the turkey who lives on the hill.

They dined on mince and slices of quince,

Which they ate with a runcible spoon,

And hand in hand on the edge of the sand

They danced by the light of the moon,

the moon, the moon,

They danced by the light of the moon.